© Edizioni Arka, Milano, 2001

First published in the United States in 2001
by Watson-Guptill Publications,
770 Broadway, New York, NY 10003
www.watsonguptill.com

Library of Congress Catalog Card Number: 2001093579

ISBN: 0-8230-5580-9

First published in Italy in 2001
by Edizioni Arka, Milano

Printed in Italy by Fotoriproduzioni Grafiche E. Beverari, Verona

First printing, 2001

1 2 3 4 5 6 7 / 07 06 05 04 03 02 01

Web site for Bimba Landmann:
www.bimbalandmann.com

Nicolo's Unicorn

Story by Sylvaine Nahas
Illustrations by Bimba Landmann

Watson-Guptill Publications / New York

Nicolo stares out of his
bedroom window. He watches the
sun rise slowly behind his
neighborhood in Venice.

"Nicolo, why aren't you ready for
school yet?" asks his older brother.
"What are you daydreaming about?"

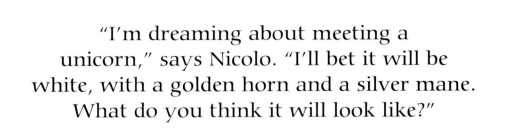

"I'm dreaming about meeting a unicorn," says Nicolo. "I'll bet it will be white, with a golden horn and a silver mane. What do you think it will look like?"

"Don't be silly," says his brother. "You know there's no such thing as a unicorn. Now stop daydreaming and let's go or we'll be late!"

At school, Nicolo watches the trees
outside blow softly in the wind.

"Nicolo, why aren't you reading
along with us?" asks his teacher.
"What are you daydreaming about?"

"I'm dreaming about meeting a
unicorn," says Nicolo.
"I'll bet it will be able to run very
fast. Do you think it will let
me ride on its back?"

"Don't be silly," his teacher says.
"You know there's no such thing as
a unicorn. Now stop daydreaming
and pay attention!"

Nicolo sits at his kitchen table.
He watches the rain beat,
pitter–patter, against the window.

"Nicolo, why haven't you finished
your dinner?" asks his mother.
"What are you daydreaming about?"

"I'm dreaming about meeting a unicorn,"
says Nicolo. "I'll bet it will eat
tiny magic white flowers. Do you
think it will let me taste one?"

"Don't be silly," says his mother.
"You know there's no such thing as a
unicorn. Now stop daydreaming
and finish your vegetables!"

Nicolo sits on a bench in the park.
He watches the boats in the pond
rock back and forth.

"Nicolo, why aren't you playing
with your friends?" asks his aunt.
"What are you daydreaming about?"

"I'm dreaming about meeting a unicorn," says Nicolo. "I'll bet it will like to swim. Do you think it will let me play with it in the water?"

"Don't be silly," says his aunt. "You know there's no such thing as a unicorn. Now stop daydreaming and go have some fun!"

Nicolo looks at the moon.
The stars are twinkling brightly,
far away and quiet.

"Nicolo, aren't you ready to go
home yet?" asks his aunt.
"What are you daydreaming about?"

"I'm dreaming about meeting a unicorn," says Nicolo. "I'll bet it will be able to fly all the way to the moon! Do you think it will let me come along?"

"Don't be silly," says his aunt.
"You know there's no such thing as a
unicorn. Now stop daydreaming
and let's go home!"

Nicolo doesn't want to
stop dreaming about unicorns.
The next day, he runs all the way
to his grandfather's house.

When he gets there, he is out of breath.
"What is it? What's the matter?"
asks his grandfather.
"I want to meet a unicorn," says Nicolo.
"You know lots of things. Do you know
where I could find one?"

"Yes, I do," his grandfather says.

"Look in colors and paintbrushes.
You can make unicorns appear
with your very own hands.

Look in flutes and tambourines.
You will hear them galloping in the music.

Look in the books you read.
You will find a unicorn lurking
behind every page."

"Your unicorn *does* exist, Nicolo.
It can gallop a million miles an
hour in your imagination.
In your heart, it can fly to the
moon and back a thousand times.
Don't ever stop looking,
even when you're all grown up.
Don't ever stop dreaming about
meeting a unicorn."